The Sand Dragon

by Su Swallow

illustrated by Silvia Raga

ZERO TO TEN

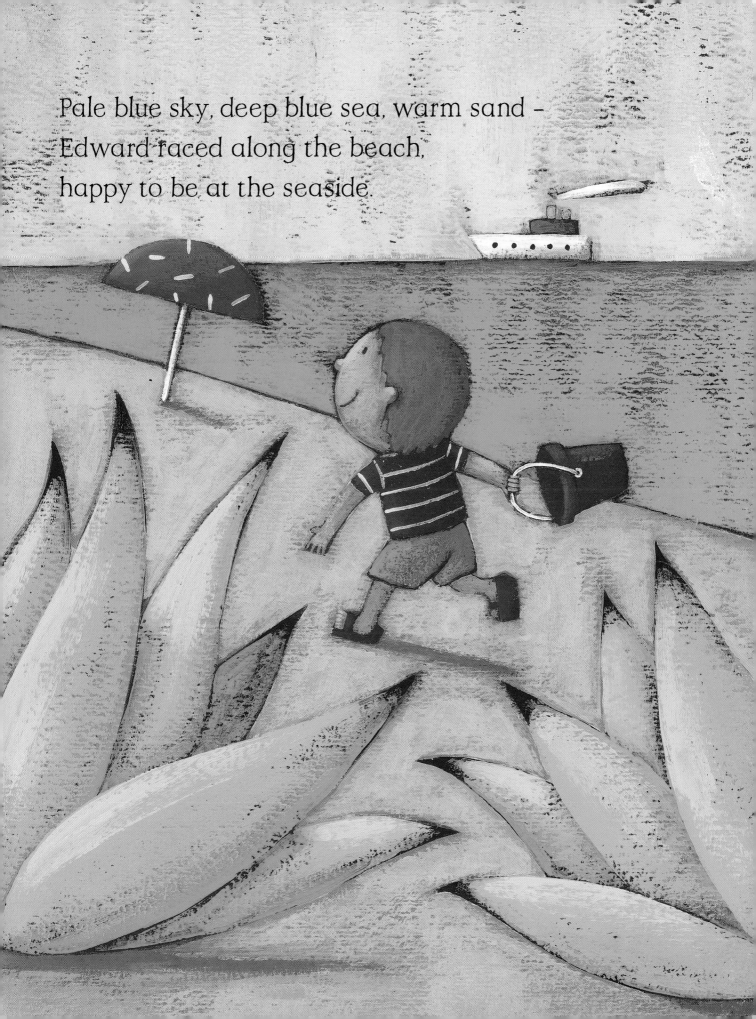

Pale blue sky, deep blue sea, warm sand –
Edward raced along the beach,
happy to be at the seaside.

Splish splash, splish splash!
The boy bobbed along
with his boat.

On the beach, Edward
searched for treasure.
He found shells –
thin ones and fat ones,
sharp ones and smooth
ones and shells like
wide slippery fans.

'This one is for you,' he said.

Hurrah! Castle complete.
Hard work, building a castle
out of sand.

Time for a rest.
Time to draw.

'What's that?' asked Mum,
as Edward drew in the sand.

'It's a sand dragon.'

'Say goodbye to sand dragon.
It's time to go home now.'

The sun went down.
The waves splashed on the shore.
The sand dragon lay on the beach.

As the tide rose, the sand dragon slipped into the water, and floated under the stars.

He dipped below the
waves and swam
among the seaweed,
nibbling the tasty fronds
as he explored the
watery world of the sea.

He danced and frolicked with the
sea creatures.

When it was time to go back, the sand
dragon let the waves carry him back
to shore.

The dragon lay on the sand to dry
and dream of his underwater adventures.

Edward came back, ready for
another day at the seaside.

What was that lying on the sand?
'Mummy, my sand dragon hasn't
moved all night!'